First published in hardback in Great Britain by
HarperCollins *Children's Books* in 2017.
First published in paperback in 2018.

HarperCollins *Children's Books* is a division of HarperCollins
Publishers Ltd. Text and illustrations copyright © Rob Biddulph 2017
The author / illustrator asserts the moral right to be identified as the
author / illustrator of the work. A CIP catalogue record for this book
is available from the British Library. All rights reserved.

Visit our website at www.harpercollins.co.uk

ISBN: 978-0-00-820742-7
Printed and bound in China
10 9 8 7 6 5 4 3 2 1

For Kitty.
And Cleverin.

Written and illustrated by

RobBiddulph

HarperCollins *Children's Books*

This is Sid Gibbons.   And this is his mum.

And this is the reason they're looking so glum.

(Sid's dinner was up on the table before,
But now it's an upside-down tea-on-the-floor.)

This isn't the first time
that Sid's been in trouble:

On Monday his ball turned the bird bath to rubble.

On Tuesday his pens were left out to go dry.

On Wednesday his bedroom looked like a pigsty.

Mum folded her arms as she spoke to the lad.
"Now Sidney, remember the talk that we had?"
But Sid, he was hatching a plan in his head,
And before she could finish the little chap said...

"I didn't do it! I'm Innocent Sid.
But if you'll just listen I'll tell you who did.
Kevin! Y-yes, that's right, Kevin. He did it.
Why don't you just ask him? He'll have to admit it."

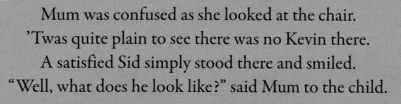

Mum was confused as she looked at the chair.
'Twas quite plain to see there was no Kevin there.
A satisfied Sid simply stood there and smiled.
"Well, what does he look like?" said Mum to the child.

"Um... he's ever so tall
and he's ever so wide.
And ever so smiley,"
the little boy lied.

"Has only one tooth.
Is as strong as a gorilla.
Has lots of pink spots
on a fur of vanilla.

"Whenever I'm down
with that sad, lonely feeling
He comes down to stay
through the hatch in my ceiling.

"He's kind but he's clumsy
and that, I'm afraid,
Is why he's to blame for
the mess that's been made."

Mum rolled her eyes and her cheeks went bright red.
"That's enough Sidney. Now, please go to bed.
And have a good think 'cos these fibs have to end –
you must not blame *your* mess on a make-believe friend!"

Grumpily Sid made his
way up the stairs
And put on his PJs
(the ones with the bears).

He sat in the darkness,
his mood not improving
When slowly the door
to the hatch started moving.

Suddenly light flooded
in through the chink
Which Sid could have sworn
was vanilla and pink.

Excited and nervous
all at the same time
He took a deep breath
and he started to climb.

When he got to the top, what a sight to behold!
Just look at that sky – what a fine shade of gold.
The tree trunks were purple, the leaves made of jelly.
The flowers were huge and incredibly smelly.
The clouds were all star-shaped, the rainbow was dotty.
The ladybirds stripy, the bumblebees spotty.
The grass was a carpet of mint-green and yellow.
And who's this familiar sort of a fellow?

"Kevin? You're Kevin!" said Sid with a squeal.
"I cannot believe that you're actually real!
You're just like my drawing! No need to pretend.
We'll play every day. You can be my best friend."
Kevin just smiled and took Sid by the hand,
and they started to walk through this magical land.

They passed lots of beasties
that looked pretty silly.

Some hairy.   Some slimy.   Some leggy.   Some frilly.

Sid smiled and said, "Hi!" as each one came toward him,
But oddly, the strange-featured creatures ignored him.
Big Red, Little Blue, the one shaped like a kidney,
They nodded to Kev, but they looked straight through Sidney.

By the time they had rocked up at Kevin's front door
The facts of the matter were hard to ignore.
Here in Kev's world, as I'm sure you are seeing,
'Twas Sidney who was the imaginary being.

CHEZ KEVIN

Now I have to report, with a slight note of dread,
That Sidney was hatching a plan in his head.
A plan oh so cheeky, so tricksy, so clever...

Invisible Sid = Bestest fun ever!

Are you catching my drift? Do you see what I mean?
You can't get told off if you cannot be seen!

So... Sid scribbled on walls and he scribbled on floors.

He bounced on the beds and he swung from the doors.

He hosed down the dog and he frightened the hens.

He left all the lids off of Kevin's new pens.

And when it was teatime, invisible Sid...
Well, look to your right and you'll see what he did.

Just as Kev started to
clean up the floor
In walked his dad
through the wrecked
kitchen door.

Slowly, but surely,
his cheeks went bright red.
"That's enough Kevin,
now please go to bed!"

It was then that Sid noticed as Kevin walked by
A single blue tear welling up in his eye.

Suddenly Sidney did not feel so clever.
He actually felt like the least best-friend ever.
He went up the stairs full of sorrow and guilt
To where he found Kevin tucked under his quilt.

"Kevin," Sid whispered, "Oh, Kevin stop crying.
I've been really selfish, there is no denying.
I'm terribly sorry I've got you in trouble,
I'm going to put right all my wrongs at the double."

So... Sid scrubbed all the walls and he scrubbed all the floors.

He mended the bed and he fixed all the doors.

He brushed down the dog and he settled the hens.

He tidied away all of Kevin's new pens.

And then he gave Kevin a card that he'd made.
"My drawing is not very good I'm afraid.
But I hope that you like it and find in your heart
A way to be friends like we were at the start."

Kevin just smiled and he gave Sid a cuddle,
And there they both stood in a big teardrop puddle.

Kevin showed Sid the way back to the hatch.
They said their goodbyes as Sid unhooked the latch.
But before he went down a reformed Sidney Gibbons
Collected some flowers and tied them with ribbons.

Back in his room Sidney got himself dressed
Then ran down the stairs, flowers clutched to his chest.
He dashed through the house from one room to another.
At last, in the kitchen, our Sid found his mother.

"Mum, I am sorry for causing such trouble.
I am the one turned the birdbath to rubble.
I messed up my room and *I* ruined my pens.
I should not blame it all on my innocent friends."

Then Sidney gave her the beautiful posy,
And Mum was so happy her cheeks went all rosy.

Now, this is Sid Gibbons.

And this is his mum.

And there on the slide's our invisible chum.

Since Sid learned his lesson
and stopped blaming others
Kevin and him have been
closer than brothers.

I wonder if you have a make-believe friend.
An invisible pal upon whom you depend.
If no-one believes you don't grumble or moan,
'Cos one thing's for certain...

...You're not on your own.